The Rape of Bunny Stuntz

A Play in One Act

by A.R. Gurney, Jr.

A Samuel French Acting Edition

SAMUEL FRENCH

FOUNDED 1830

New York   Hollywood   London   Toronto

SAMUELFRENCH.COM

Copyright © 1964 by Albert R. Gurney, JR.

STORY OF THE PLAY

An efficient suburban matron, chairing an evening meeting, finds that she has to cope with a strange, off-stage intruder who claims he knows her. The meeting degenerates step by step into a wild party, even as the intruder becomes increasingly insistent and insulting to the leader. Ultimately, the lady finds herself confessing to the lure of a liaison with this representative from the under side of society, and by going off with him, she manages to appease whatever it is that tears groups apart. The meeting ends by coming to order under a new woman, but the implications are that she, too, will have to go through some sort of expiation, and that the ritual must be repeated again and again.

CAST OF CHARACTERS

BUNNY STUNTZ, *a woman of about 35.*
HOWIE HALE, *a man of about 40.*
WILMA TRUMBO, *a woman of about 30.*

DESCRIPTION OF CHARACTERS

Bunny Stuntz: a bright, efficient, and attractive woman, anywhere from twenty-five to forty-five. She wears a dress or suit.

Wilma Trumbo: should be cast in contrast to Bunny. Heavier or lighter, shorter or taller. Preferably younger. She should have a more rumpled appearance, and a more naive, wide-eyed stance.

Howie Hale: a hale fellow, well met. Anywhere from thirty to fifty. Wears a suit or a sports jacket.

SETTING

The action takes place at an evening meeting in an indeterminate meeting hall—a school, a club, a theatre. The play can be put on anywhere that meetings might be held: a theatre stage, an auditorium, even a room. All it needs is a table with a chair behind it, and perhaps an American flag behind that.

The Rape of Bunny Stuntz

We see a small table, with a chair behind it, facing the audience. After a moment, BUNNY STUNTZ *comes briskly up onto Stage from the audience. A claque of APPLAUSE accompanies her. She carries a square metal box. Pinned on her chest is an unusually large round name-tag which reads "Hi! I'm Bunny Stuntz!" She clicks around behind the podium and places the box neatly in front of her, squaring it with the edge of the table. As the APPLAUSE dies down, she smiles at the audience.*

BUNNY. Hi! I'm Bunny Stuntz! (*Looks around brightly.*) And I want to welcome all you newcomers to our meeting tonight. I'm sure that before the evening is over, we'll have the opportunity to know each other much, much better. (*More seriously.*) I also want to thank all of you—veterans, shall we say—for electing me chairman last week. I will try to do my best tonight, and in the months ahead. Now: to business— (*She smiles again, and briskly tries to open the box in front of her. It doesn't open. She struggles with the catch. No result. She smiles at the audience.*) I must have locked this— (*Pause. Then in a whisper.*) Purse— (*She snaps open her purse and fumbles in it. No result. Pause. Another whisper.*) Pin— (*She reaches into her hair and removes a bobby pin, tries it in the lock. No result. She bangs the box on the table, always sweetly, and then shakes it a couple of times. No result.*) Why, I could have sworn— (*She looks out over the audience, shading her eyes.*) Is Howard Hale out there? Howie, are you out there, please?

HOWIE. (*Who has been standing in the rear.*) Right here, Bunny!

BUNNY. Howie, would you come up here a moment?

(HOWIE *comes up onto Stage, bright and eager. On the lapel of his coat is also a name-tag: "Hi! I'm Howie Hale!" He smiles self-consciously at the audience, perhaps nods or waves to a couple of familiar faces.*) Howie, I think I forgot the key to this thing. (HOWIE *looks at* BUNNY, *looks at the box, and then putters with it, while* BUNNY *speaks to the audience.*) This is Howie Hale. If you want to have anything *done* around here, ask Howie.

HOWIE. (*To* BUNNY.) It's locked.

BUNNY. I think it is. Yes. I must have left the key home.

HOWIE. Let's go on, anyway. Let's go on without it.

BUNNY. With*out* it? (*Pause.*) No, we can't, Howie. No, we really can't. (*Smiles at audience.*) If you'll bear with us, people. (*To* HOWIE.) No, Howie. Everything's in here. The minutes from last week, the agenda for this week, the mailing list, the money—everything. (HOWIE *looks at her, then reaches in his pocket, takes out his own key ring, examines a bunch of keys; he begins trying them on the box with great dedication.*) Oh, it won't open with just any old key, Howie. *That* I know. . . . It requires a special key, I'm afraid. (*To audience.*) Oh darn it. This is an inauspicious beginning for my maiden voyage, isn't it? (*To* HOWIE, *who is having no success with his keys.*) Howie, I know where the key is. I left it home. Now it comes back. It's in a cubbyhole in my desk, actually.

HOWIE. In a cubbyhole?

BUNNY. Exactly. In my desk. Now look, Howie— (*She fumbles in her purse, takes out piece of paper and a ballpoint pen.*) Call Bill. . . . Here's the number— (*She writes down the number, then smiles at the audience.*) My husband Bill's sitting with our three kiddo's— (*Back to her writing.*) And Howie, tell him to look in the third cubbyhole from the right—third from right—and get the key—which has a tag on it—tag—and then to bring it over. . . . Tell him to get Debbie Bayliss from next door—here's her number—just say Debbie, he'll know—

and Debbie can stay with the kiddo's while Bill brings the key over here. (*She folds the paper neatly and hands it to* HOWIE.) Would you do that, Howie?

HOWIE. (*Saluting her.*) Yavohl, mein capitan! (*He exits into the audience and out.*)

BUNNY. (*Calling after him.*) You're a peach, Howie. (*To audience.*) He's a peach. I hope you all get to know Howie before we're through. He's a do-er. (*Pause. She straightens the box on the table.*) Well. It will be about ten minutes, people. I apologize. I'm terribly sorry. The best laid plans gang oft agley. I think I locked this thing because of the kiddo's, and after supper, I was in such a hurry to *get* here that I must have forgotten the key. (*Pause. She taps her teeth with her pen.*) Why—while we're waiting—are we here? Is it fair to ask that? I think it is. I was thinking of tonight, as I left my family: why? Why have so many of us, from so many different walks of life, left our homes, our comfortable chairs, those easy—routines which we all have at the end of a busy day—why do we leave all that, to come here? It costs money to come here. I know that. The group has to charge its dues, of course, and when you add on the sitter's fees, and the gas and depreciation to *get* here, and perhaps even a dinner out—why, I can imagine that it has cost some of us a good ten dollars, in toto, to come here. And yet we are here, you and I, all in this thing together. Why? (*She smiles.*) Certainly you didn't come here just to see me. Just to see a lady forget her key. . . . No, you expect things to happen here tonight, don't you? And they will! I can promise you that. We'll go somewhere, if I have anything to do with it. Because— (*A CAR is heard, faintly, Off Left; she stops, listens.*) Do I hear someone tooting outside? I think I do. I think someone's tooting his horn out in the parking lot. (*She shades her eyes, looks out over the audience.*) Wilma Trumbo, do I see you by the door? Wilma, would you just run out to the parking lot and find out what's what? Thanks, Wilma. You're a peach. (*To audience.*) It

sounded like a familiar horn. I suspect it was my husband
Bill. With my key. He might have thought of it, all by
himself. And dashed over with it. He's very thoughtful.
Quiet, uncomplicated, thoughtful. He encourages me to
be active. He'd be here himself, but he's terribly tired.
He travels all the time, and so when he's home, naturally
he wants to rest. But he gives me my head. That's the
point. "Fulfill yourself," he says. "Go on. More power
to you." . . . And so here I am, standing up here in
front of all of you. (*Pause.*) But why here? What is ful-
filling about all of this for all of us? That's the question
we still have to sink our teeth into. And that's the question we should be chewing and digesting at the moment.
I mean, we're not just here to be enter*tained*. We could
get that, staying at home, watching our boob tubes. No.
All of us here—no matter what our race, creed, or color—
all of us are in some way unhappy people. Oh not un-
happy-unhappy. Heaven forbid! . . . Just—discontented
—concerned—and so: involved. Oh, we have rich full lives
at home. Or in the marketplace. I don't mean that. I just
mean—I just mean that what goes on there is not *enough*.
Husband, children, home—they just don't—fill the gap,
do they?

(WILMA TRUMBO *calls softly from halfway up the aisle.
    She is younger than* BUNNY, *with frillier clothes.
    She too wears a badge: "Hi! I'm Wilma Trumbo!"*)

WILMA. Bunny, may I speak to you for a moment?
BUNNY. Of course, Wilma. Come up here. . . . This
is Wilma Trumbo, everyone. (WILMA *joins* BUNNY *Onstage, and whispers something in her ear.* BUNNY *steps
back.*) Why, that's the silliest thing I ever heard, Wilma.
WILMA. That's how I understood it, Bunny.
BUNNY. (*Looks at* WILMA, *then laughs.*) I think we
should share this news item with our friends, Wilma.
(BUNNY, *with her arm around* WILMA, *brings her Downstage and speaks to the audience.*) People, Wilma says

that there's a man out there in the parking lot in a red car—

WILMA. (*To* BUNNY.) A red Impala—-

BUNNY. A red Impala, who has been fuh-rantically tooting his horn because he claims— Oh, you tell them, Wilma—

WILMA. (*To audience.*) He says he's waiting for Bunny.

BUNNY. (*Laughing.*) Waiting for me!

WILMA. (*To audience.*) For Bunny Stuntz.

BUNNY. (*To audience.*) All right, now, who knows anything about this? Who's trying to be funny? Is this some—secret initiation for your new chairman? . . . Seriously, we've got a long way to go tonight. Who knows anyone belonging to a red—what is it, Wilma?

WILMA. Impala.

BUNNY. Impala. I've got a date, now, with an Impala yet. . . . Describe him, Wilma. I'll figure out who it is. (*To audience.*) Or one of you can.

WILMA. (*Hesitatingly; to audience.*) I couldn't see him very well—it was dark out there, in the parking lot. . . . He had a jacket on—a leather jacket, because it sort of glistened—and a sort of whispering voice—and he was chewing gum. . . . I don't know. I never saw him before. (*A pause.*)

BUNNY. Oh, Wilma, you make him sound so *menacing*. (*To audience.*) Doesn't Wilma sound scary? (*More seriously.*) No. He sounds like some—teen-ager, trying to be funny. Some teen-ager. We ought to have a place where teen-agers can *go*. I have a note on that, right in this box. (HOWIE *comes onto the Stage.*) Yes, Howie?

HOWIE. Bill can't find the key, Bunny.

BUNNY. Oh, now, Howie—

HOWIE. He looked everywhere while I stayed on the phone.

BUNNY. It was in the cubbyhole in my—

HOWIE. He looked there, Bunny.

WILMA. Maybe you lost it, Bunny.

BUNNY. I did not lose it, Wilma. I do not lose things! (*She remembers the audience; smiles.*) I don't lose keys.

HOWIE. Let's go on, anyway, Bunny. Let's play it by ear.

WILMA. Yes, Bunny—

BUNNY. (*Holding the box.*) I hate to do that. I really hate to do that. (*To audience.*) Everything—everything's in here. All the previous minutes, the money, all the proposals for tonight. I had everything all worked out. I had divided up the topics. I had divided up all of us. I had group captains—Howie, you were one, and Wilma, so were you. It's all here. In this box. The whole thing. (*To* HOWIE, *more softly.*) Did Bill look in the bedroom for the key?

HOWIE. He said he looked everywhere, Bunny.

BUNNY. (*A touch of bitterness.*) I'll bet he didn't look in the bedroom. Knowing Bill. (*Pause.* WILMA *and* HOWIE *look at her, waiting for a decision. She looks at them, at the box, at the audience, then comes to a decision.*) I'll whip home. It will take me fifteen minutes at the most. (*To audience.*) People, why don't you talk quietly among yourselves? Raise issues, ascertain facts, hammer out modes of action.

HOWIE *and* WILMA. Aw, Bunny—come off it—

BUNNY. (*To audience.*) People, I really don't think I can be of much good to anyone without that key.

HOWIE. Can we break out the coffee, down in the cafeteria?

BUNNY. But we have so much to do!

HOWIE. We can do it over coffee.

WILMA. Yes. That's right. Coffee now. Instead of later.

BUNNY. (*Pondering.*) Will you *promise* me, all of you, that you'll stay within the general lines of our purpose? I mean, coffee breaks can get so—chatty. Will you promise me you'll try to get something done, albeit informally, over coffee?

HOWIE. Oh, sure, Bunny.

BUNNY. (*Suddenly and determinedly.*) Howie, go down

and start the coffee. (*To audience.*) But those of you who want to stay here in your seats for a more formal program can do so. Wilma can be discussion leader. (HOWIE *salutes her, and bustles off into audience.*)

HOWIE. C'mon, gang. Anyone for coffee? (*Exits.*)

(WILMA *settles nervously into* BUNNY'S *seat behind the table.*)

BUNNY. All set, Wilma?

WILMA. (*Meekly.*) I guess so—

BUNNY. (*Appraising her.*) Beautiful! Meanwhile, back to the ranch! (*She picks up her box, and starts off Left, then stops, clutching the box; to* WILMA.) Who's that out there?

WILMA. (*Looking off Left.*) Where?

BUNNY. (*Low, to* WILMA.) There's somebody slouching out there in the shadows. (*To audience.*) There's somebody slouching out there in the wings.

WILMA. (*Looking.*) I think it's him.

BUNNY. You think it's who, Wilma?

WILMA. I think it's the man with the Impala.

(*Pause.* BUNNY *squints, looking off Left.*)

BUNNY. All right, all right. Who's there? (*Pause.*) Who are you out there, please? (*Pause. She turns to audience.*) Whoever is out there is being very, very silly, indeed. Frankly. (*Back to Left.*) Will you come in, please, and make yourself known? . . . Will you come in, please? (*Pause.*) Wilma, would you go ask him, please, to come in? (WILMA *nods and exits Left, a little warily.* BUNNY *turns to the audience, still clutching the box.*) Why, this is the limit, isn't it? I mean, he's just slinking around out there, like a—snake. (*She turns back to the Left, fascinated.* WILMA *comes back in.*)

WILMA. He wants you, Bunny.

BUNNY. Oh. He wants me, does he? (*She speaks to*

the Left.) Well, he's not going to get me till he comes into the light. (*To audience.*) Is he? (*To* WILMA.) If he wants to join the meeting, then he's welcome to come right in and join it. (*To audience.*) Isn't he? (*To Left.*) Sir, if you want to join the meeting, then you're welcome to join us. It's an open meeting. I had it announced as such. There are plenty of new people here. From all walks of life. (*To audience.*) Aren't there? (*Back to Left.*) You can come in and sit down, or you can go down in the cafeteria and have coffee. Either one. I'm Bunny Stuntz. I'm chairing this meeting, and I'll be glad to talk to you personally right after I whip home and get the key to this box. (*She starts off in the other direction, to the Right, as if to exit through the audience. Then she stops.*) Wilma, give him a name-tag.

WILMA. I left them at the door, Bunny.

BUNNY. Then here— (*She takes off her own name-tag.*) He can turn this around. (*She takes her ball-point pen out of her purse.*) Tell him he can write his name on the back of this. (*She hands* WILMA *the name-tag and the pen.* WILMA *exits Left.* BUNNY *speaks to the audience.*) He should identify himself. As we all have. (*Pause.*) I feel so—naked without my—fig-leaf. (*She smiles.*) But I think you all know me pretty well by now. (*She takes another step or two, as if to leave, but seems fascinated by what is happening off Left.*) I know what this is all about. I've seen it happen, oh, many times. Some people are terribly, terribly shy. They want to join groups, and yet they find it terribly difficult. They go through all sorts of peculiar maneuvers. First they throw away our notices. Then they drive by the place, but don't come in. Then they *come* in and stand on the side-lines. *Finally*, especially if someone takes them in tow, they join, and they generally end up being one of the most active participators. You watch. (WILMA *comes in from the Left, slowly.*) What happened, Wilma?

WILMA. (*Holding out two halves of the name-tag.*) He tore it up.

BUNNY. (*Taking the two halves.*) He tore it *up?* (*She tries to piece the two halves together, vaguely.*)

WILMA. I gave it to him with the pen, and I said, "Please write your name on the back." And he snatched it away, and tore it up, and handed back the pieces. He put the pen in his pocket.

BUNNY. Oh, now, *honestly.* (*She looks off Left, then turns to audience.*) He's just *standing* there.

WILMA. He's not a teen-ager, either. He's got five o'clock shadow.

BUNNY. Did he *say* anything? (*To audience, smiling nervously.*) Does it *speak?*

WILMA. Yes, he said one thing, when he handed back the mutilated name-tag.

BUNNY. And what was that, pray tell?

WILMA. He said he had the key. (*Pause.*)

BUNNY. (*Slowly, with great intensity.*) He has no key.

WILMA. All I know is what he said, Bunny. (*To audience.*) I'm just reporting what the man said.

BUNNY. (*More briskly again.*) He does not have my key. My key's at home. How could he possibly have the key? I'm going home right now to *get* the key. (*She starts again to exit into the audience, then stops, braces herself, and steps a little toward the Left. She speaks very slowly to the Left.*) How could you possibly have the key, sir? (*Pause, while she listens. She takes a step closer.*) What? (*Another pause, another step; then she turns to* WILMA.) He whispers. He hisses. I can't hear a word he says.

WILMA. I heard one word.

BUNNY. What word? What word?

WILMA. Hotel. (*Pause.*)

BUNNY. Ho—

WILMA. —tel.

BUNNY. Hotel? Ho-*tel?* What hotel? I don't know anything about hotels. I don't go to hotels. (*Calling out Left.*) What do you mean, hotel? (*Pause; she turns to* WILMA.) I still can't hear a damn thing he's saying.

WILMA. Maybe he's saying you left the key in a hotel. (*Pause.*)

BUNNY. (*Slowly; to audience.*) The man is mad. The key is home.

WILMA. Shall we call the police, then?

BUNNY. (*To audience.*) The man is stark, raving mad.

WILMA. Should we get Howie and some of the men to throw him out?

BUNNY. (*To the audience.*) The only hotel I've been in in *years* was last May when I went down to New York with Rosie Rinehart to see the James Baldwin thing. (*To* WILMA.) That's the only hotel room I've been in in years, Wilma. (*To audience.*) When I go anywhere, I go with friends. Or with my family. And we stay with friends. We have friends all over the eastern seaboard. Friends from school, friends from college, friends from Bill's business. Why, I don't think we *ever* fall back on hotels or motels or things like that. Lonely, sleazy rooms. Never.

WILMA. Oh, I know it, Bunny. Oh, I know it. Knowing you, I can believe it. Knowing you.

BUNNY. (*She glances at* WILMA *peculiarly, and then looks off Left.*) What's he doing out there? Is he twirling something on the end of a chain? What's he twirling? I can't see.

WILMA. (*Looking out.*) It's the key.

BUNNY. It is *not* the key! . . . It is not the key.

WILMA. Do you suppose he's trying to hypnotize you, Bunny?

BUNNY. (*Snapping out of it, looking away from Left.*) Ignore him, Wilma—I said, ig*nore* him, Wilma. (WILMA *snaps out of it;* BUNNY *speaks to audience.*) Ignore him, everybody. Ignore him. I'm going to ignore him. He's an—exhibitionist, obviously. He wants a fuss, and when he doesn't get one, he'll go away. So just forget that there's anybody out there. Just—ignore him. (*She cradles the box in her arms.* HOWIE *comes Onstage from the* *audience. His coat is off, and he hides a can of beer behind his back.*)

HOWIE. Hey, Bun! Get the key yet?

BUNNY. No, Howie. We were—delayed.

WILMA. Howie, there's a—

BUNNY. (*Quickly.*) Never mind, Wilma. . . . We were delayed, Howie. Let's leave it at that. (*She notices he is hiding something.*) What's that, Howie?

HOWIE. (*A little defiantly, holding out the beer.*) That's beer.

BUNNY. Beer?

HOWIE. Yeah. Beer. Someone broke out some beer, down in the cafeteria. And there's a piano there. Doc Feldstein's playing sing-along songs from our college days.

WILMA. (*Clapping her hands.*) Oh, what fun!

BUNNY. (*After a glance at* WILMA.) Howie, I don't understand this. I don't think we are here to have a party.

HOWIE. Yeah, well what the hell?

BUNNY. (*Indicating audience.*) I don't think all these people are here, Howie, simply to drink beer and sing outmoded songs.

HOWIE. (*With feeling.*) Yeah, well maybe we better skip the key. (*Then, guiltily.*) We had nothing to *do* down there, Bun. I dunno. We got nervous. Sort of uneasy. . . . So we're having a party.

(*Pause.* BUNNY *looks from* HOWIE *to the audience to the box to off Left.*)

BUNNY. I have decided—not to bother with the key. . . . I'll try to remember the agenda. (*Takes another pen and notebook out of her purse.*) Howie, you and I and Wilma can quickly jot down a few notes so that we'll have something to go on. I mean, there's no point in being completely *random*.

HOWIE. (*Leaving the Stage.*) Um—give me a yell when you're ready to roll, Bun.

BUNNY. Howie—

HOWIE. (*Singing, imitation operetta singer.*) "Tell me, pretty maiden, are there any more at home like you?" (*He exits.*)

WILMA. (*Continuing, softly, longingly.*) "There are a few, kind sir . . ." (*She peters out.*)

BUNNY. (*She looks at* WILMA, *glances off Left, then speaks half to* WILMA, *half to audience.*) Anyone who wants to go down to the cafeteria *can*, you know. I mean, if that's what you want. If that's what you came for. Musical comedy. I myself am just going to jot down a few quick topics for those who are just interested enough to stick it out. (*She goes to the chair.*)

WILMA. (*A little wistfully; looking out at the audience.*) Lots of people are going down, Bunny.

BUNNY. (*Beginning to write on a piece of paper.*) Would you like to go, Wilma? Tell me the truth. (*To audience, smiling nervously.*) I mean, what *am* I? A slave-driver? A *dict*ator? (*To* WILMA.) If you want to go down there, you should go, Wilma. (*With a glance off Left.*) I can handle things by myself.

WILMA. No, I'll stay. I'll help you. (*She stands behind* BUNNY'S *chair.*)

BUNNY. (*Writing.*) Now. Well. Let's see. I had broken the thing down into goals. Immediate goals, A; and far-reaching goals, B.

(*From off Left, the sound of MUSIC, cool jazz, insinuating, without a vocal. Both* WOMEN *look up and off.*)

WILMA. He's got a transistor radio.

BUNNY. (*Setting her jaw.*) I had set up three major committees, Wilma. A fact-finding committee, a ways-and-means committee and— (*The MUSIC becomes louder.* BUNNY *has to shout to be heard.*) and an ultimate objectives committee. I thought that Howie could be chairman of— (*She stops, closes her eyes, puts down her pen, then stands up and strides toward the Left.*) Would you turn that off, please? (*The MUSIC continues.*) I said, would you turn that *off*, please! We are having a meeting here. (*The MUSIC plays a little longer, then cuts out.*) Thank you so much. (*Pause. The MUSIC starts again, loud.* BUNNY *shouts it down.*) ALL RIGHT! (*The MUSIC stops.*) We will talk, you and I. (*To audience, a little sarcastically.*) He and I will comm-*u*-nicate.

WILMA. Oh, Bunny—

BUNNY. (*Dryly.*) It's all right, Wilma. I think it's trying to tell us something. (*To off Left.*) *Ser*-iously, sir, you think you know me, but you have made a mistake. We have never met. We have never crossed paths or swords or anything else. Period. (*Pause.*) Never. Never, never, never. I'm sorry. No. It's not true.

WILMA. (*Wide-eyed, to audience.*) He's just smiling. I can see his teeth.

BUNNY. (*To off Left.*) No sirree, bub. I'm sorry. (*Pause.*) And no, that's not my key. I said that is not my key. No. (*Pause.*) No it is not. No. Would you please go away.

WILMA. Bunny, let's get some men up here.

BUNNY. I can handle this, Wilma.

WILMA. (*To audience.*) She seems to think she can handle this.

BUNNY. (*To off Left.*) All right then, *when* have I seen you before? Speak. Can you speak? You know, words and things. (*Pause.*) When? Names and dates, please. Chapter and verse.

WILMA. Oh, Bunny, don't bother.

BUNNY. I have to pin this thing *down*, Wilma. (*To audience.*) It's the only way he'll go away. (*To off Left.*) When have we . . . met? (*Pause.*) Name a day. Any day. Monday, Tuesday, Wednesday. January, February, March. Go on. Name a day.

WILMA. (*To audience.*) He's just—shrugging his shoulders. And scratching.

BUNNY. (*To* WILMA.) All right, Wilma. *You* pick a day.

WILMA. Me?

BUNNY. Since apparently he won't. Pick any day you want. I can account for it.

WILMA. Oh, Bunny, please—

BUNNY. Name a day, Wilma!

WILMA. (*Weakly.*) Tuesday.

BUNNY. Tuesday. Good. (*To off Left.*) Wilma thinks we met on a Tuesday. At what time, Wilma?

WILMA. Bunny, I didn't say you met— (*To audience.*) I didn't say—

BUNNY. At what *time,* Wilma?

WILMA. (*Cowed.*) Three P.M.

BUNNY. Good. So on Tuesday afternoons, at 3:00 P.M., I met this character in a hotel. Some foul, sleazy hotel, apparently, where you can bring in women. . . . And where I suppose I gave myself to him in a moment of sublime surrender and then left my key. . . . Oh, this is ridiculous.

WILMA. Of course it's ridiculous.

BUNNY. (*Walking away from Stage Left.*) Now Wilma, tell him where I am on Tuesday afternoons.

WILMA. All right. (*She goes to Stage Left; calls out.*) Mrs. Stuntz couldn't possibly have been with you on Tuesday afternoons because on Tuesday afternoons she— (*Turns to* BUNNY.) Where *are* you on Tuesday after-noons?

BUNNY. You know, Wilma. (*To audience.*) Wilma knows.

WILMA. (*To audience.*) I *don't.* I really don't. I've forgotten.

BUNNY. On Tuesday afternoons, I drive Binkie all the way over to Westfield for his art lesson, *and* do the marketing, *and* drive back.

WILMA. Is that true?

BUNNY. Of course it's true, Wilma.

WILMA. Oh, I know it's *true;* I just hadn't heard it before.

BUNNY. I take Marge Jackson's little girl, too. I take

Pammy Jackson. (*Looks out into the audience.*) Marge Jackson, are you out there? Would you come up and tell this man what I do Tuesday afternoons? Would you tell him where I take your very talented little Pammy? (*Pause.*)

WILMA. I think Marge is down singing college songs.

BUNNY. *I'll* tell him then.

WILMA. Oh, I'll *tell* him, Bunny. I believe you. I just didn't know you did that on Tuesday afternoons.

BUNNY. Well, I do. I've saved all the paintings. There's one of a dragon.

WILMA. I just didn't know, that's all. (*She goes to the Left.*) Mrs. Stuntz couldn't possibly have—

BUNNY. Would he like to see my calendar? I'll show him my engagement calendar. It has everything marked down on it since January one. Everything I've done. Meetings, coffees, carpools, dentists, errands, everything. (*Calling off Left.*) Would you like to see that? Would that convince you that you've made a mistake? I think if you looked at it— (*To audience.*) I think if he looked at it, he'd realize that there's not a single time in my life that I could have possibly— (*Back to Left.*) gone with you to some seamy, sleazy hotel. You can look at my calendar. Anybody can. I'm perfectly willing to make it public. It's right here in this— (*Goes to box, realizes that it is locked.*) box. (*Pause.*)

WILMA. It doesn't make any difference, Bunny—

BUNNY. (*Bitterly.*) It seems everything important in my life is locked in this box.

WILMA. (*Looking off Left.*) He's holding out the key, Bunny.

BUNNY. (*Shaking her head.*) That's not the key. The key's at home. With Bill and the children. It's on the table by my bed.

WILMA. (*Looking off Left.*) He's nodding—as if he knows that table, Bunny.

BUNNY. He does not know that table.

WILMA. (*Looking off Left.*) He's nodding as if he

knows that bed. (BUNNY *stiffens, looks at* WILMA, *and strides off Left.* WILMA *watches anxiously. There is the sound of a loud SLAP.* WILMA *gasps. Then two more SLAPS come in quick succession.* BUNNY *comes reeling backwards onto the Stage, holding her cheek, looking back Offstage.*) Why, he— (*To audience.*) Let's have some *men* up here, for heaven's sake! She's—

BUNNY. (*Grimly.*) No, I'm all right. (*To audience.*) I said I'm all right.

WILMA. (*Starting off toward the audience.*) I'm going to call the police! He hit you!

BUNNY. (*Sitting down.*) That was because I hit him. (*To the Left, sneeringly.*) Like some cheap, second-rate blonde in a B movie, I'm now resorting to slapping strange men. I've slipped to that level, apparently.

WILMA. Oh, Bunny, let's have him thrown out!

BUNNY. (*Talking to the Left.*) Oh, sure. And you think that will get rid of him for good? Oh, I know this kind of character. He'll be on my neck for life unless I beat him my own way. He'll pull up alongside of me at traffic lights; he'll call on the telephone. Sly, cheap, insinuating, like a snake. And I've got to stare him down.

(HOWIE *rushes on from the audience, now looking thoroughly rumpled, perhaps with lipstick on his face; he now carries a glass half full of liquor. He grabs* BUNNY *by the waist.*)

HOWIE. (*Singing, as he spins* BUNNY *around.*) "And if there's one thing worse . . . in this universe . . . it's a woman . . . I said a woman . . . I mean a woman without a man . . ." (BUNNY *breaks away.*) C'mon down, Bun. We got a great party.

WILMA. Oh golly! Just what the doctor ordered!

HOWIE. Sure! Listen! Doc Feldstein's playing shady songs on the piano. Marge Jackson's doing a way-out dance on a table. And me, I've been introducing myself to a newcomer in the corner!

BUNNY. Oh, Howie, Howie. You've all let go, haven't you?

HOWIE. Naw, Bun, we've all caught *on*. But we need you. C'mon down, Bun.

BUNNY. (*Shaking her head.*) I'm sorry, Howie. No.

HOWIE. We need an anchor man, Bun.

BUNNY. (*With a glance off Left.*) No.

(HOWIE *looks at her; then begins to sing a suggestive popular song to her, shuffling lewdly around her. He ends up with his arm around* WILMA, *who giggles sheepishly. Then he rushes off.*)

WILMA. Oh, Bunny, let's join the party. (*To audience.*) All of us. Let's all join the group downstairs. It sounds like such fun. (*To* BUNNY.) Please, Bunny. You're not getting anywhere up here. It's too late to get started on a meeting. . . . Our friends are down there, Bunny. Song and laughter and casual, harmless sex-play. (*To audience.*) We're all being party-poops, those of us who are left. Life goes on without us, down there, while we fuss around up here, worrying about some stupid man. There comes a point when we can become too serious, too obsessed with things. Come on. (*To* BUNNY.) Come on, Bunny. Fill the cup, seize the hour, join the dance! (BUNNY *shakes her head, staring out Left.*) I'm going, Bunny. I feel like a good, stiff drink. And a little music. I'm going to join my friends. Are you coming? (BUNNY *again shakes her head.*) Goodbye then, Bunny. (WILMA *exits through the audience;* BUNNY *suddenly turns and gasps.*)

BUNNY. Oh, Wilma— (*Pause. She looks out over the audience, shading her eyes; by now, the LIGHTING has become stark and theatrical. She stands in a harsh pool.*) Has she gone? . . . She has gone. . . . Anybody left? I can't see very well. These lights—any familiar faces out there? Any? Oh there *must* be! . . . . And anybody who is still here is my friend. I mean it. You're my friends, out there, whoever you are, because you came here and you stuck it out. . . . (*She takes a deep breath, glances toward Left, and then pulls her chair Downstage front. She sits in it, quietly. She speaks musingly, ironically—never sentimentally.*) So I'm going to be frank with you, friends. Since you stayed, I'll be frank. What if—what if I *have* seen this man before? What if—last Tuesday, for example—I *didn't* take Binkie to his art lesson? What if I was in the front of the house—gardening, say—cultivating my own garden—when he—this creature—happened to drive by in his red—Impala? What if his car makes such a racket that I naturally look up, and see this creature in his leather jacket, bombing by? Suppose he waves to me, and maybe I wave back, or *half* wave, uncertain, not knowing who he is. Suppose he drives around the block, thinking I've—what is that awful expression?—"given him the eye"? Back he comes, and there I am, crouched in the petunias. And so he pulls up to the curb, and I get the picture, and walk into the house, slamming the door. And the poor sap has had these dreams of glory ever since, till finally he follows me down here, and tries to embarrass me in front of all my friends at a public meeting. (*Stands up; speaks to Left.*) Now, so long, sonny boy. (*Back to audience.*) There. That's it. That's my confession. I'm admitting what could, possibly, have happened. Now perhaps we can at least arrange for our next meeting. (*She goes to the table, starts to open her purse. Pause. Glances Left, then back at audience. The LIGHTS are a little brighter on her now. She sits on the edge of the table.*) He's still there, friends. . . . All right—we'll take it farther. Try this one. Suppose I go into the kitchen. Suppose there's a good, big, fat leg of lamb in the oven, and I tritty-trot in there to baste it. Suppose Bill is, per usual, away and suppose the children are still at school. Suppose this character appears at the kitchen window, and leers at me, until I ask him please what in hell does he want. As if I didn't know. (*She speaks to Left.*) Oh. You want to use the telephone? No, I don't think that's possible. I'm sorry, no. So please go away. (*Pause, as she glares off Left.*) Or—why not? I mean, there are neighbors around—friends, just like you people, out there, and the knife for the leg of lamb is handy—and I'm a little bored. So—yes. You may use the telephone. Come in. It's right here in the kitchen. . . . Don't you want to use it after all? I didn't think so. Get out then. Now. (*Pause. She watches Left, then turns to the audience. She has to peer against the light.*) He won't go, friends. He's still standing there. (*Takes a deep breath.*) All right. Picture this, if you will. (*Speaks to Left.*) He's still there, slouched in my kitchen, leaning against the counter, chewing gum— (*She closes her eyes.*) And I am somewhat attracted to him. I'm admitting this. I'm making this public, which is apparently what I'm supposed to do. Dig we must, as they say— (*To audience.*) And all of you know what I mean, because you're the ones who came and stayed—to see. You want to see what's there, too, don't you, waiting in the wings? So all of us here, all of us in this room tonight, are a little in love with what is dark and shoddy and unpleasant. Yes. And I think it's good that we admit these things. Yes. I feel much better now that it's all out in the open. Recognizing the thing is—dealing with it, and of course then driving it out. (*She draws herself up proudly. Speaks to Left.*) So sure. Yes. O.K. I'll admit out loud that I am attracted. And I'll even admit that in my own house—while we stood eyeing each other—something—physical might have happened— (*Long pause as she stares off Left; then she shakes her head and turns again to audience.*) I said, something might have happened in that vacuum if the sounds of the world hadn't come flooding in. Here come the clichés, people, but thank God for clichés, say I. . . . Suppose just then I hear two children fighting over a truck. Or I hear the Millworths' boxer barking at the mailman. And I shake my head. I say, "Thanks but no thanks." And I say to that man, "Get out, or I'll scream for all my friends!" And he gets out. But fast! (*She smiles at the audience*.) So there it is, isn't it? It's all out in the open. I've lied, I've told the truth, I've made a public confession of a nightmare. And now he should go. That's it. That's all. There isn't any more. I have values. So do you. We believe in things. We have families, friends, rules we can count on. We can afford to turn our backs on the—dark, seamy side of things. (*She turns her back on Stage Left*.) So let's go. Back to our homes. Back to our clean houses which are better than grubby hotel rooms. And we'll drive back in station wagons which really *do* make more sense than red Impalas: I mean, who do we want to im*pale*, anyway? Oh, I believe in these things so strongly. I believe that attractive people are more attractive than unattractive people. I believe that children, with haircuts, in polo coats, going to see their grandmother are more important than some cheap, cheap, cheap disgusting tussle with a strange man. I believe— (*She grabs the box off the table*.) I believe in everything here. What I've done. What I'm doing. What I hope to do. I believe in continuity and organization. I believe in a community of intelligent, responsible citizens, like you and me. So let's all, all go home! (*Pause. She closes her eyes*.) But it's not enough, is it? (*Puts box on table*.) I'm still here. (*Glances off Left*.) And he's still there— (*Squints out at the audience*.) And you're still here. . . . (*Perhaps a SPOT on her now, isolating her as she stands alone. She shields her eyes with her hand, and then suddenly lets her hand drops. She stares out into the light, slowly shaking her head*.) Oh, people— Oh, my friends. . . . (*She lets out her breath in a long sigh*.) Hi. I'm Bunny Stuntz. And you're still here because you want to see the rape—of Bunny Stuntz. (*Pause. Silence. Then, from the Left, a KEY on the end of a cheap, shiny chain is tossed out onto the Stage, at her feet. She picks it up and dangles it out in front of the audience*.) See? See, friends? Can everyone see? It's a key. On the end of a chain. Snake-like, ain't it? (*She looks at the key,* *imitates a housewife in an advertisement.*) A key! Why, Bill, it's just what I needed! I've wanted one for so long. How ever did you guess? It's so smartly styled, so attractively priced! Wait, wait! Let's see whether it works on this exquisite little box I happen to have here— (*She trots to the box, inserts the key, turns it in the lock.*) Well whadya know, gang? The crummy little thing does the trick! (*She holds the box out to the audience, like a priestess, and slowly tips it forward. It is empty.*) Empty. That's also what you wanted, isn't it? (*She puts the box formally on the table, still open. She speaks coldly, bitterly.*) Famous last words now follow: I have been found damned in birth, damned in marriage, damned in my desires. . . . Pray undo this button. . . . It is a far, far better thing I do. . . . Gently, sir, it's mother's day. . . .

(*She exits Left, walking slowly, like a bride. Immediately, the sound of raucous LAUGHTER, as* WILMA *enters tipsily, carrying a glass of liquor.* HOWIE *leaps out at her from Stage Right. Both are in disrepair.*)

WILMA. (*Caught and laughing.*) Howie, now stop it! I'm a married woman!

HOWIE. (*Grabbing her shoulders.*) You threw your doorkey into the center of the room, kid. I got it. See? (*He holds out the key.*)

WILMA. (*Sensuously.*) I know, Howie, but sweetie, that was just a game. . . . (*She glances around.*) Where's Bunny? (*Pause.* WILMA *peers off Left.*) I feel a draught. . . . The outside door is open. . . . (*She slides toward Left.* HOWIE *watches. From off Left, we hear the sound of a CAR starting and roaring off.* WILMA *turns to* HOWIE *slowly, straightening her dress.*) Bunny Stuntz is dead.

HOWIE. (*After a pause.*) You mean, she's—?

WILMA. (*Holding out her hand for her key.*) Dead. To us.

HOWIE. You mean, just because she's—?

WILMA. (*Holding out her hand.*) Dead. (HOWIE *drops her key into her hand.* WILMA *turns to the audience, speaks very efficiently.*) People: I regret to announce that Bunny Stuntz is dead. Now. Well, Howie, run down-stairs and tell Marge Jackson to put on her clothes and drink black coffee. Then get on the telephone and call Bill Stuntz. Be tactful, Howie, and understanding. Then tell Doc Feldstein to hightail it on over to Bill's with a sedative. (HOWIE *runs off into audience.* WILMA *picks up* BUNNY'S *box.*) And I think probably the best thing the rest of us can do is to go home calmly and quietly. I'll call you about the next meeting. Anybody who needs a ride come up and speak to me. I've got a large Ford station wagon with a rear seat which faces forward. (*She closes the box efficiently, picks it up with* BUNNY'S *purse, and exits briskly into the audience as the HOUSE-LIGHTS come up.*)

END

PROPERTIES

Large name tags (worn by all three characters)
Metal box (carried on by Bunny)
Purse (carried on by Bunny)
Key ring (brought on by Howie)
Ballpoint pen (used by Bunny)
Can of beer (brought on by Howie)
Key on a long chain (tossed on stage)
Glass of liquor (brought on by Wilma)

SKIN DEEP
Jon Lonoff

Comedy / 2m, 2f / Interior Unit Set

In *Skin Deep*, a large, lovable, lonely-heart, named Maureen Mulligan, gives romance one last shot on a blind-date with sweet awkward Joseph Spinelli; she's learned to pepper her speech with jokes to hide insecurities about her weight and appearance, while he's almost dangerously forthright, saying everything that comes to his mind. They both know they're perfect for each other, and in time they come to admit it.

They were set up on the date by Maureen's sister Sheila and her husband Squire, who are having problems of their own: Sheila undergoes a non-stop series of cosmetic surgeries to hang onto the attractive and much-desired Squire, who may or may not have long ago held designs on Maureen, who introduced him to Sheila. With Maureen particularly vulnerable to both hurting and being hurt, the time is ripe for all these unspoken issues to bubble to the surface.

"Warm-hearted comedy … the laughter was literally show-stopping. A winning play, with enough good-humored laughs and sentiment to keep you smiling from beginning to end."
- TalkinBroadway.com

"It's a little Paddy Chayefsky, a lot Neil Simon and a quick-witted, intelligent voyage into the not-so-tranquil seas of middle-aged love and dating. The dialogue is crackling and hilarious; the plot simple but well-turned; the characters endearing and quirky; and lurking beneath the merriment is so much heartache that you'll stand up and cheer when the unlikely couple makes it to the inevitable final clinch."
- NYTheatreWorld.Com